Don't Let the Pigeon Stay Up Late!

Oh, good, it's you. Listen, it's getting late and I need to brush my teeth. Can you do me a favor?

Don't Let the Pigeon Stay Up Late!

words and pictures
by mo willems

Don't Let the Pigeon Stay Up Late!

words and pictures by mo willems

SCHOLASTIC INC.

New York Toronto London Auckland Sydney
Mexico City New Delhi Hong Kong Buenos Aires

For Trixie at bedtime

ISBN-13: 978-0-545-04180-5
ISBN-10: 0-545-04180-5

Text and illustrations copyright © 2006 by Mo Willems. All rights reserved. Published by Scholastic Inc., 557 Broadway, New York, NY 10012, by arrangement with Hyperion Books for Children, an imprint of Disney Children's Book Group, LLC. SCHOLASTIC and associated logos are trademarks and/or registered trademarks of Scholastic Inc.

12 11 10 9 8 7 6 5 4 3   7 8 9 10 11 12/0

Printed in the U.S.A.   40

First Scholastic printing, September 2007

Thanks.

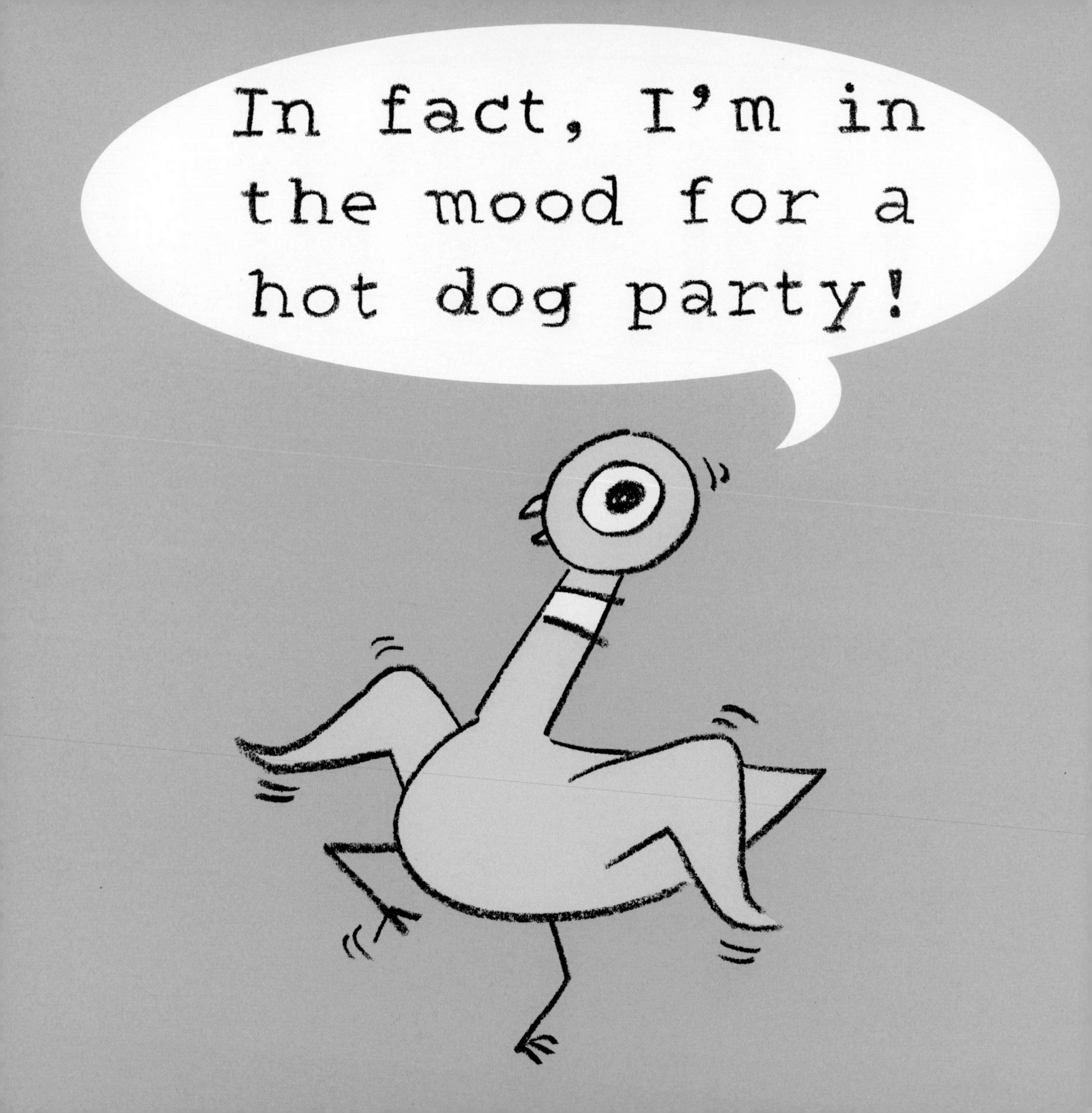
In fact, I'm in the mood for a hot dog party!

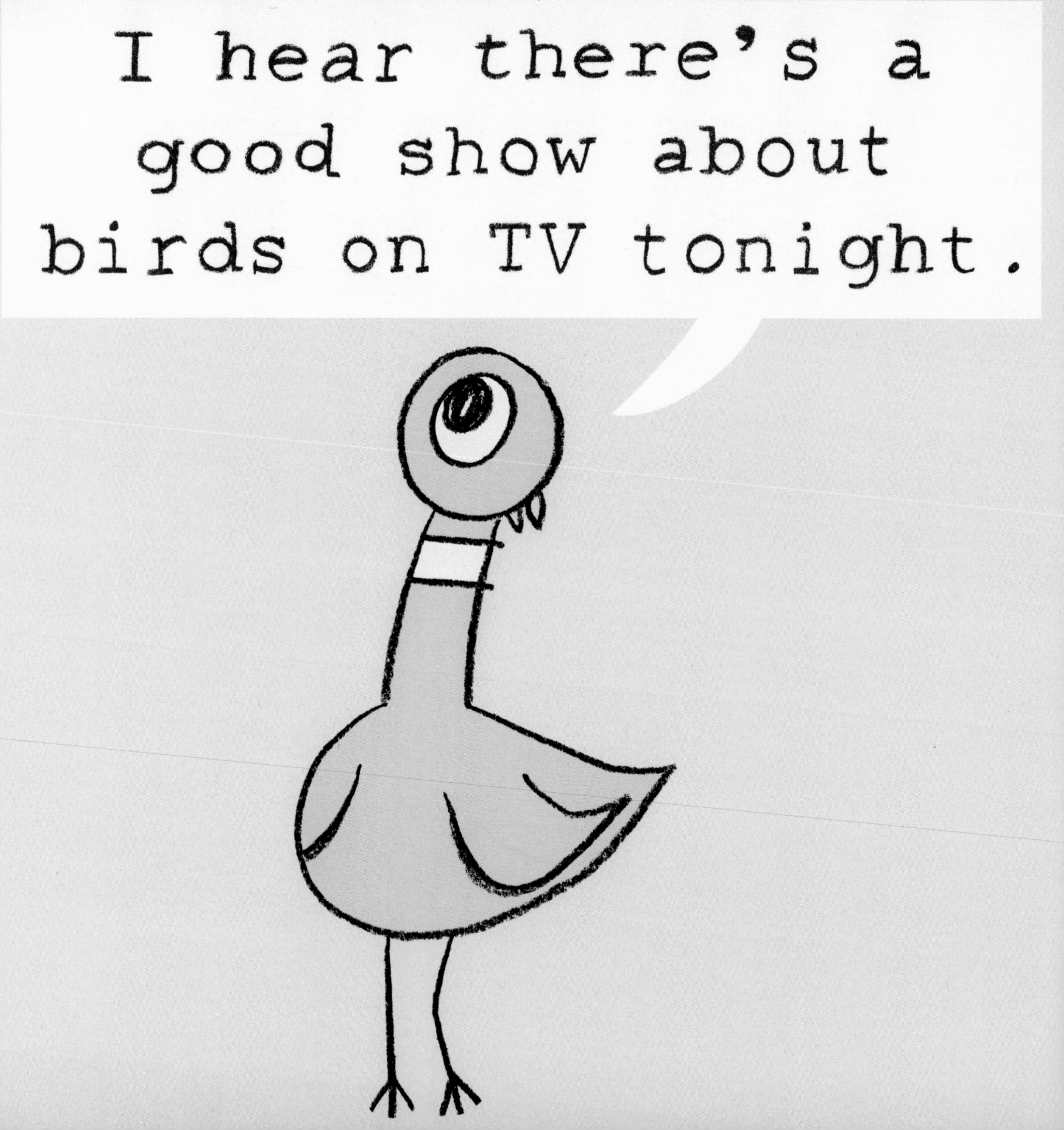
I hear there's a good show about birds on TV tonight.

Can I have a glass of water?

Studies show that pigeons hardly need any sleep at all!

It's the middle of the day in China!

I'll go to bed early tomorrow night instead!

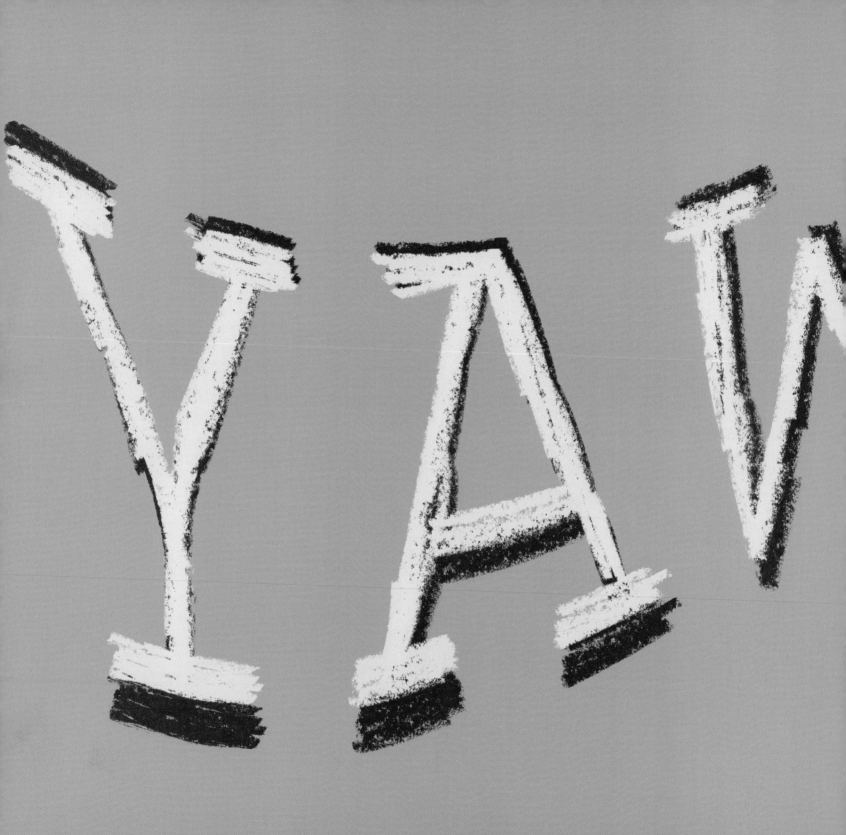

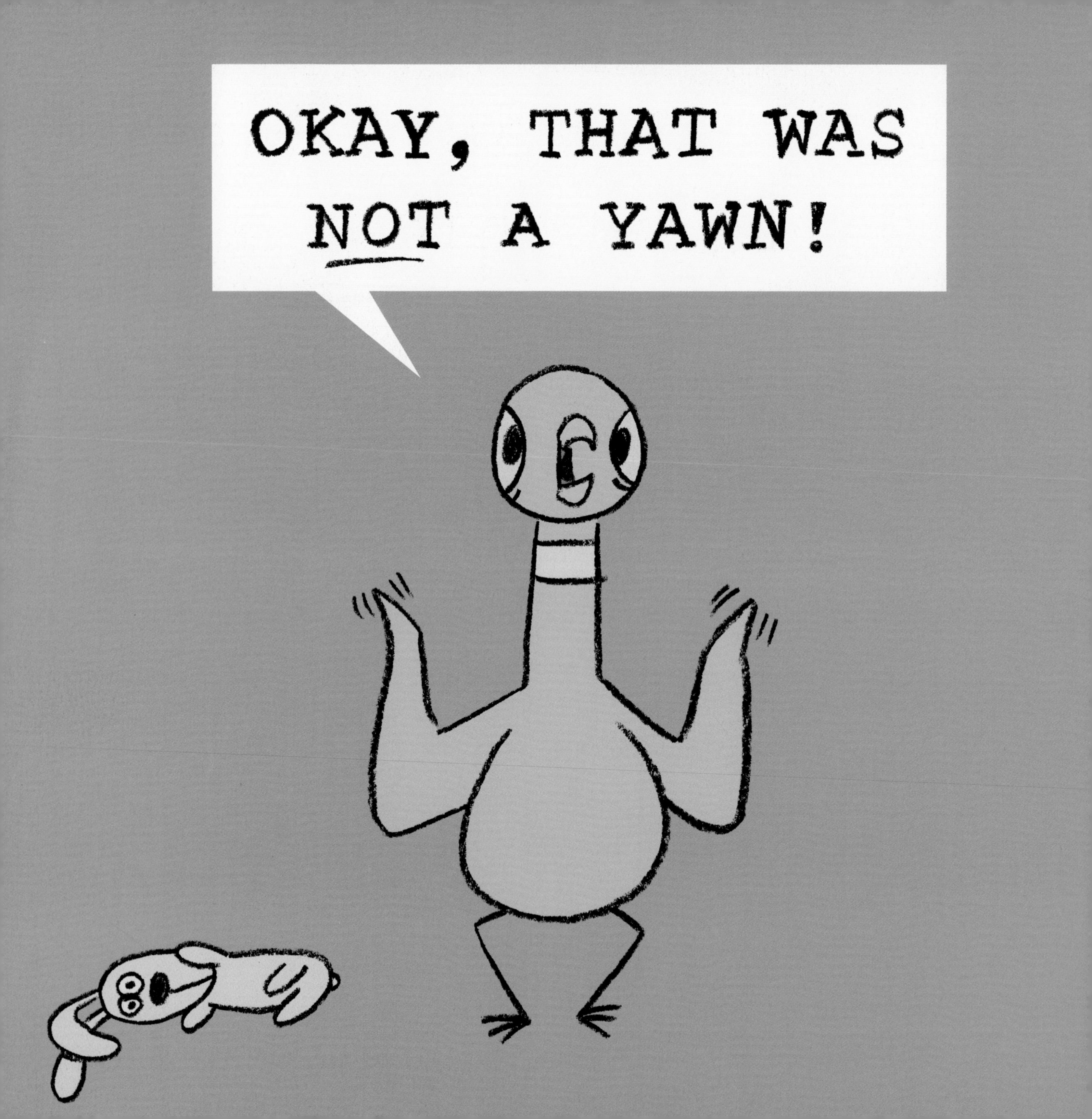
OKAY, THAT WAS NOT A YAWN!

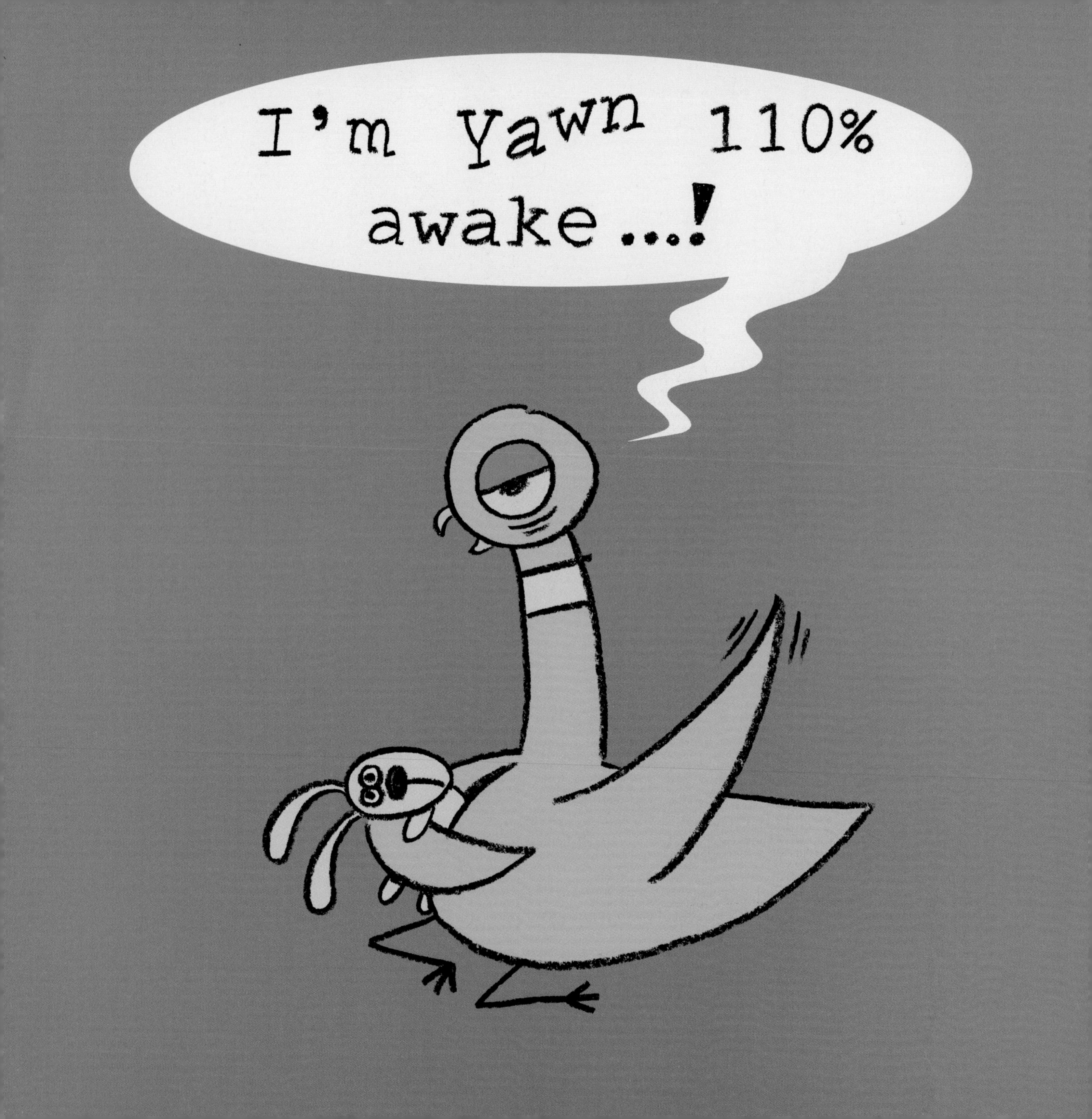
I'm Yawn 110% awake...!

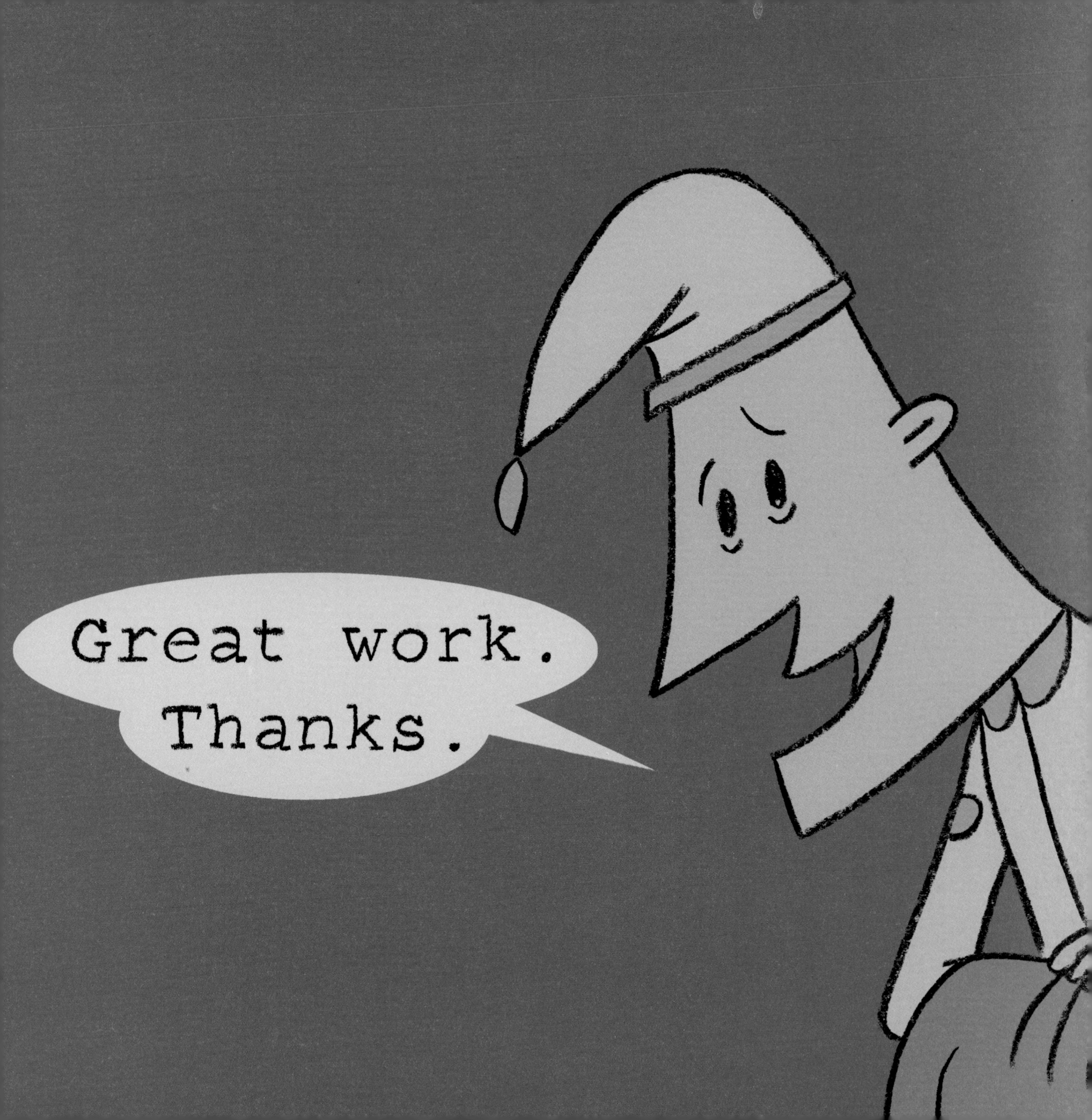
Great work. Thanks.